Mr.
TOD'S
TRAP

Mr. TOD'S TRAP

Malcolm Carrick

An I CAN READ Book

HARPER & ROW, PUBLISHERS

Mr. Tod's Trap
Copyright © 1980 by Malcom Carrick
All rights reserved. No part of this book may be
used or reproduced in any manner whatsoever without
written permission except in the case of brief quotations
embodied in critical articles and reviews. Printed in
the United States of America. For information address
Harper & Row, Publishers, Inc., 10 East 53rd Street,
New York, N.Y. 10022. Published simultaneously in
Canada by Fitzhenry & Whiteside Limited, Toronto.
First Edition

Library of Congress Cataloging in Publication Data
Carrick, Malcolm.
    Mr. Tod's trap.

    (An I can read book)
    SUMMARY: A clever but male chauvinist fox finally
trades places with his wife so his family won't starve.
    [1. Sex role—Fiction.   2. Foxes—Fiction]
I. Title.
PZ7.C23452Mi   1980   [E]   79-2012
ISBN 0-06-021113-X
ISBN 0-06-021114-8 lib. bdg.

To Joanne Louise

Mr. Tod was making toys for his cubs—

Elsie, Arnold, and Maurice.

"You are so clever," said Mrs. Tod.

"And you tell such great stories,"

said Elsie.

"Tell us a story

about when we were little

and Mom found the secret door

to the rabbits' home,"

begged Arnold.

"And you built our kitchen

over it," added Maurice.

"Well!" Mr. Tod grinned.

"Every day one or two rabbits

came out their secret door.

8

Your mom was there

to grab them

before they could warn

the rabbits inside."

Maurice rubbed his tummy.

"What happened then?" he asked.

Mr. Tod sighed.

"The rabbits stopped coming."

"Why?" asked Elsie.

"Because they moved away,"

Mrs. Tod told them.

"Now Daddy has to hunt

in the cold, wet fields."

9

"Not today," said Mr. Tod.

"But there is no food in the house,"
cried Mrs. Tod.

"What!" cried Mr. Tod.

"I went hunting yesterday.
I even missed the cubs' bedtime."

"I know," sighed Mrs. Tod.

"But you didn't catch anything."

"I nearly did," said Mr. Tod,

"but night came,
and you know I hate the dark."

"It's not dark now," said Mrs. Tod.

Mr. Tod looked out

at the cold, wet fields.

"But it is raining," he said.

Mrs. Tod took off her apron.

"I don't mind the rain," she said.

"Why don't *I* go hunting?"

"Because you are a woman,"

shouted Mr. Tod,

"and a mother.

Your place is here at home,

looking after the cubs.

I will go out hunting."

"Will you be back by bedtime?"

asked Elsie. "To tuck us in."

"And to play games

and tell us stories,"

Arnold added.

"We can eat supper together,"

said Maurice.

"I will be home before bedtime,"

Mr. Tod promised.

He kissed them all good-bye

and hurried off

to the rabbit fields.

Weasel was there already.

"It's so cold here," moaned Mr. Tod.

"I keep warm by chasing rabbits,"
Weasel told him.

Mr. Tod smirked.

"*I* use clever ideas
to catch rabbits," Mr. Tod said.

"What sort of ideas?" Weasel asked.

"Well," said Mr. Tod, "here is one.

"*You* chase the rabbits toward the river,

and *I* will hide by the bridge."

"Why?" asked Weasel.

"Because rabbits don't like to swim.

20

They will use the bridge,"

said Mr. Tod.

"How clever!" said Weasel,

and rushed off to look for rabbits.

Mr. Tod went to the bridge.

It was cold and wet.

Mr. Tod shivered until dusk.

"It's the cubs' bedtime now."

He sniffed. "I must go home

before it gets dark."

22

"I will make rabbit traps

that will *hold* the rabbits

when I am at home."

"To tuck us in at bedtime,"

said Elsie.

"And to tell us stories

and make us toys,"

said Arnold.

"And we will have plenty of food,"

said Maurice.

His tummy rumbled.

Mrs. Tod hugged her hungry cubs

and put them to bed.

26

"Daddy is home!" cried Elsie.

"Story time!" cheered Arnold.

"Suppertime!" yelled Maurice.

"Did you catch anything?"
asked Mrs. Tod.

"Yes," said Mr. Tod, "a cold."

"Shall I go and get a rabbit
from Weasel?" asked Mrs. Tod.

"No!" roared Mr. Tod.

"I will not accept charity.
Tomorrow I will catch a rabbit
with my new idea."

"What is that?" asked Mrs. Tod.

25

Mr. Tod went to the bridge.
It was cold and wet.
Mr. Tod shivered until dusk.

"It's the cubs' bedtime now."
He sniffed. "I must go home
before it gets dark."

They will use the bridge,"

said Mr. Tod.

"How clever!" said Weasel,

and rushed off to look for rabbits.

Mr. Tod worked all night and all day.

Then he set the traps in the fields.

"They look like toys," said Weasel.

"You watch," said Mr. Tod.

The rabbits came.

They played with the traps

until they fell asleep.

"How clever," cried Weasel.

"Now they are easy to catch."

Weasel rushed for the rabbits.

"They remind me of my cubs."

Mr. Tod sniffed.

He ran home to his family.

"Daddy is back!" cried Elsie.

They all hugged each other.

"Did the traps work?"

asked Arnold.

"Yes!" Mr. Tod beamed.

"Weasel caught a lot of rabbits."

"How many did you get?"

asked Maurice,

licking his lips.

Mr. Tod blinked.

"None," he said.

"But we are hungry," cried Mrs. Tod.

"Don't worry," Mr. Tod said.

"I have an idea for making

the greatest trap in history.

It will catch so many rabbits,

we will have a *feast*."

Mr. Tod went to work at once.

He worked day and night.

"I miss Dad's hugs," Elsie sobbed.

"I miss his stories," said Arnold.

"And I miss my supper,"
moaned Maurice.

"Hush," said Mrs. Tod.

She brought them their supper.

"This rabbit tastes so good,"
said Elsie.

"Where did it come from?"
asked Arnold.

Maurice just ate.

"Shh," Mrs. Tod said in a whisper.

"Don't tell Daddy."

In the morning Mr. Tod yelled,

"My great trap is ready. Look!"

It was a HUGE WOODEN RABBIT.

Mrs. Tod and the cubs

and Weasel all stared at it.

"Help me push it to the fields,"

cried Mr. Tod.

"How does it work?" asked Mrs. Tod.

"You will see," said Mr. Tod.

When it was in place,

he climbed inside

through a trapdoor.

"Bolt the door," he called out.

"But…" began Mrs. Tod.

"Hush, woman. This is men's work!"

said Mr. Tod.

Weasel said to Mrs. Tod,

"Take your cubs home.

I will stay

and see what happens."

Weasel bolted the door.

After a while, the rabbits came.

They stared at the wooden rabbit.

"Where did it come from?"

asked one rabbit.

"It's so huge," said another.

"Let's take it to our secret home,"

said an old rabbit.

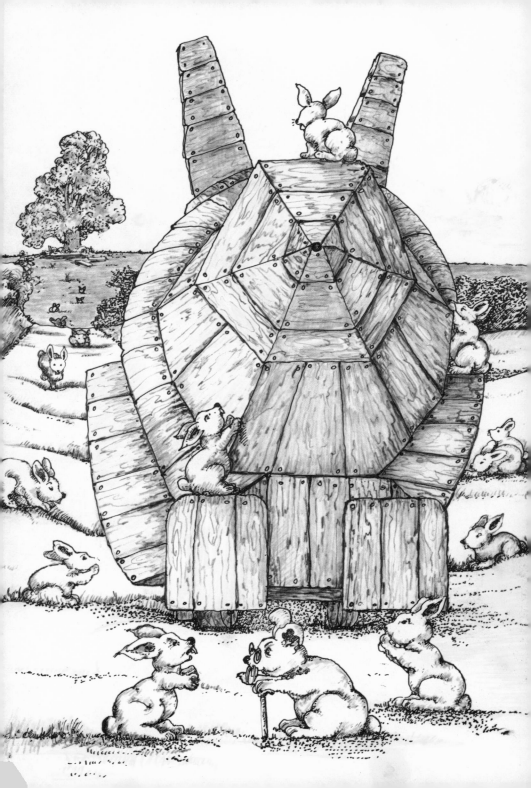

"I knew they would,"

Mr. Tod said to himself.

"Rabbits always stick together."

The rabbits pushed

the wooden rabbit home.

When it stopped moving,

Mr. Tod looked out a peephole.

There were HUNDREDS of rabbits

all around.

Mr. Tod waited until they were asleep,

then he crept to the door.

But the door was locked

FROM THE OUTSIDE.

"Oh, no," cried Mr. Tod.

"*I* am trapped.

Help! HELP!"

He howled and kicked.

The rabbits were so scared

they all ran outside

where Weasel was waiting.

He caught a lot of rabbits.

He ran to tell Mrs. Tod.

46

"It works, Mrs. Tod!

Mr. Tod is a wonder."

"But where is Mr. Tod?"

asked Mrs. Tod.

"Oh," said Weasel,

"in the rabbits' secret home

in the old oak field."

"I must go to him

before it gets dark," said Mrs. Tod.

"Look after the cubs till I get back,"

she told Weasel, and rushed off.

She found the rabbits' secret home

and the wooden rabbit.

She unbolted the trapdoor.

"Oh, it is so dark in here,"

Mr. Tod moaned.

Mrs. Tod pulled him out.

Mr. Tod stared

at the empty rabbits' home.

"Not one rabbit," he sniffed.

"Not *one* of my ideas works.

I am a flop."

"No," said Mrs. Tod. "You are clever,

a fine fox, and a great father."

"But I can't catch rabbits,"

sobbed Mr. Tod.

"Don't cry, please," said Mrs. Tod.

"I can catch rabbits for us."

"How can you?" cried Mr. Tod.

"You are only a woman."

"I will show you," she said.

"You go home

and look after the cubs."

"That is women's work," said Mr. Tod.

"But you are so clever,"

said Mrs. Tod.

"You can do it."

Mr. Tod wiped his eyes.

He blew his nose and went home.

"Are you all right, Daddy?"

asked Elsie.

She hugged him.

"Here are your warm slippers,"

said Arnold.

Maurice didn't say how hungry he was.

"Tell us a story, Dad," said Arnold.

"One with a happy ending."

Mr. Tod told them stories

about when they were little.

Then they made the beds,

swept the floors,

and washed the dirty socks.

They worked and played

until Mrs. Tod came home.

"Mom!" cried Elsie.

"How did you catch

all those rabbits?"

"I had a good teacher,"
said Mrs. Tod and smiled at Mr. Tod.
That night they had a great feast.

"If your mother does the hunting,"

Mr. Tod told them later,

"I shall have to do her work."

"So you will always be here

to hug us and tuck us in

at bedtime," said Elsie.

"And to look after us," said Arnold.

"We will have supper every day,"

cheered Maurice.

"What a good idea,"

said Mrs. Tod.

"My best idea yet,"

said clever Mr. Tod.